A Day with Air Traffic Controllers

By Joanne Winne

Welcome
Books

Children's Press
A Division of Grolier Publishing
New York / London / Hong Kong / Sydney
Danbury, Connecticut

Photo Credits: Cover, p. 5, p. 9 © FPG International; p. 7 © Corbis; p. 11, 17 and 21 © Indexstock; p. 13 © Mark E. Gibson, International Stock; p. 15 © Nova Stock, International Stock; p. 19 © Ted Kawalerski, Image Bank

Contributing Editor: Jeri Cipriano
Book Design: Michael DeLisio

Visit Children's Press on the Internet at:
http://publishing.grolier.com

Library of Congress Cataloging-in-Publication Data

Winne, Joanne
  A day with air traffic controllers / by Joanne Winne.
    p. cm.—(Hard Work)
  Includes bibliographical references and index.
  ISBN 0-516-23139-1 (lib. bdg.)—ISBN 0-516-23064-6 (pbk.)
  1. Air traffic control—Juvenile literature. 2. Air traffic controllers—Juvenile literature.
[1. Air traffic controllers. 2. Occupations.] I. Title. II. Series.

TL725.3.T7 W55 2000
629.136'6—dc21

                                                                00-055563

Contents

We work at the airport.

We work high up in
a **tower**.

We are **air traffic
controllers**.

Air traffic controllers talk to airplane **pilots**.

I tell pilots when to take off.

I tell pilots when to land.

A plane has just landed on the **runway**.

I tell the pilot where to park the plane.

9

We use many **computers**.

The computers help us know what to tell pilots.

Some computers check
the weather.

This computer shows storms.

We will tell pilots where the
storms are.

13

This computer shows all the planes in the air.

I tell pilots when it is safe to land their planes.

We watch the runways.

We can see the runways
at night.

17

A plane is ready to land.

I check my computer.

I tell the pilot which runway to use.

We help pilots fly planes safely.

We like being air traffic controllers.

New Words

air traffic controllers
  (**air tra**-fik kun-**troh**-lerz) people
  who give directions to pilots
computers (kum-**pyoo**-terz)
  machines that give information
pilots (**py**-litz) people who fly
  airplanes
runway (**run**-way) a long strip
  of road planes use for take off
  and landing
tower (**tow**-er) a tall building

To Find Out More

Books
Planes
by Byron Barton
HarperCollins Children's Books

Some Planes Hover & Other Amazing Facts About Flying Machines
by Kate Petty, Ross Watton, and Jo Moore
Millbrook Press

Web Sites
Knowble
http://www.knowble.com
Check the airport section to see what it's like to fly a plane.

Off to a Flying Start
http://k12unix.larc.nasa.gov/flyingstart/module1.html
Learn about the history of airplane flying, the parts of a plane, and how planes fly.

Index

About the Author
Joanne Winne taught fourth grade for nine years, and currently writes and edits books for children. She lives in Hoboken, New Jersey.

Reading Consultants
Kris Flynn, Coordinator, Small School District Literacy, The San Diego County Office of Education

Shelly Forys, Certified Reading Recovery Specialist, W.J. Zahnow Elementary School, Waterloo, IL

Peggy McNamara, Professor, Bank Street College of Education, Reading and Literacy Program